Dayswork

ALSO BY CHRIS BACHELDER

The Throwback Special

Abbott Awaits

U.S.!

Bear v. Shark

ALSO BY JENNIFER HABEL

The Book of Jane

Good Reason

In the Little House